The Shenby num through down the
goalkeeper to beat.

'Out, Chris, out!' ca
the angle.'

Chris was distracted by the oddly familiar voice and glanced towards the cottage. He was so shocked, he barely made a move to stop the striker dribbling round him and slotting the ball into the back of the net.

'Why didn't you dive at his feet?' the man yelled as Chris still stared his way. 'You just let him waltz past you.'

Andrew noticed the look of dismay on Grandad's face. 'Er, I think you might have put Chris off a bit there, Dad . . .'

Also available by Rob Childs, and published by
Young Corgi Books:

THE BIG MATCH
THE BIG DAY
THE BIG HIT
THE BIG KICK
THE BIG GOAL
THE BIG GAME
THE BIG PRIZE
THE BIG CHANCE
THE BIG STAR
THE BIG FREEZE
THE BIG BREAK
THE BIG WIN

Omnibus editions:
THE BIG FOOTBALL COLLECTION
THE BIG FOOTBALL FEAST

Published by Corgi Yearling Books, for older
readers:

The Soccer Mad series:
SOCCER MAD
ALL GOALIES ARE CRAZY
FOOTBALL DAFT
FOOTBALL FLUKES

SOCCER AT SANDFORD
SANDFORD ON TOUR

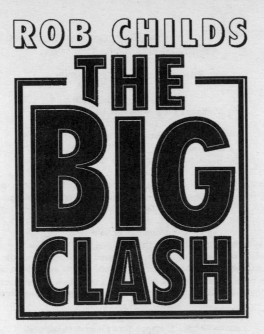

ROB CHILDS
THE BIG CLASH

Illustrated by Aidan Potts

YOUNG CORGI BOOKS

THE BIG CLASH
A YOUNG CORGI BOOK : 0 552 545333

First publication in Great Britain

PUBLISHING HISTORY
Young Corgi edition published 1998

Set in 14/18pt Linotype New Century Schoolbook

Young Corgi Books are published by Transworld Publishers Ltd,
61-63 Uxbridge Road, Ealing, London W5 5SA,
in Australia by Transworld Publishers (Australia) Pty. Ltd,
15-25 Helles Avenue, Moorebank, NSW 2170,
and in New Zealand by Transworld Publishers (NZ) Ltd,
3 William Pickering Drive, Albany, Auckland.

Made and printed in Great Britain by
Cox & Wyman Ltd, Reading, Berkshire

Especially for all goalkeepers – my own favourite position.

1 On the Way

The ball bobbled crazily about the goalmouth.

'What a scramble!'

'It's in this time – must be.'

'No! Another corner. Keeper's saved it again.'

'He's having a blinder.'

'We should be six up by now.'

The home supporters could hardly believe that their team still hadn't managed to score. Hanfield Juniors had been on top for so much of the match, but the cup quarter-final remained deadlocked at 0-0.

The corner-kick landed safely in the arms of Chris Weston, Danebridge's goalkeeper and captain, and he clutched the ball to his jersey.

'That ball's like a boomerang,' laughed Philip, their lanky central defender. 'It keeps on coming back to you.'

'Just one of those days, I guess,' Chris said with a grin. He felt in great form and was enjoying himself tremendously.

He had even saved a penalty before half-time, diving the right way to turn the kick around the post. His side were now only a few minutes away from earning a replay, but Hanfield refused to give up.

No sooner had Chris booted the ball upfield than it was back once more in his own penalty area. Philip tried to scoop it clear, but the ball fell to an attacker who chested it down and caught it sweetly on the volley.

'Goa—!' yelled one of the parents on the touchline.

The cry was choked off. There was a flash of green across the goal and in the next instant the ball changed course and flipped over the crossbar.

'Ohh! Fantastic save! That kid's unbeatable.'

Chris's grandad led the applause and turned to Danebridge's headmaster.

'How much longer to hold out?' he asked anxiously.

Mr Jones glanced at his watch. 'A couple of minutes, that's all,' he said and then shouted a warning to his team. 'Mark up tight, reds.'

They need not have worried. Chris leapt high to claim the ball from the corner, knowing that Hanfield had committed themselves fully to the attack. They'd left only two defenders back to cope with any breakaway.

The captain also knew that Danebridge had the ideal pair of

strikers to take advantage of that situation. They were both fast with good dribbling skills. One was Rakesh Patel, their leading scorer, and the other had proved equally deadly in front of goal since coming into the team after Christmas. She was Kerry Sharpe, the first girl to wear the red and white stripes of Danebridge.

Chris's long kick sailed wide to Rakesh on his right. The winger flicked the ball further ahead and gave chase, and there was no way that the chubby full-back could catch him. Meanwhile Kerry darted to the left to try and drag the other opponent away and create more space for Rakesh.

Hanfield's last defender had a problem. Should he go and challenge the winger or stay with the girl?

Forced to make a choice, he decided Rakesh was the main danger and moved over to block his route to goal.

Rakesh had to choose what to do now. He fancied taking the boy on himself, but Kerry was unmarked and screaming for the ball. If he messed up the chance, he was certain to get a mouthful from her about being greedy. He played safe. Kerry Sharpe had a tongue to match her name!

Rakesh timed his pass to perfection, slipping the ball inside as the defender lunged in to tackle. With the keeper drawn out of position to cover a possible shot from the winger, Kerry had the goal at her mercy.

She didn't bother to control the ball. She just hit it first time as it rolled across her path. It was a clean

strike, but for one awful split-second, Kerry thought it was going to miss the target. The ball veered to one side and snicked the post as it sped into the net.

The late goal came as a cruel blow for Hanfield. As Kerry celebrated with her dancing teammates, the home side stared at one another in shock that Danebridge had grabbed the vital winner. They barely had time to kick off again before the referee blew his whistle for the end of the game.

Chris felt slightly embarrassed as he shook hands with the opposing captain. 'Well played, you didn't deserve to lose today,' he said.

'Dead right, there,' the boy muttered. 'Without you, Danebridge would have been massacred.'

The players gathered around Mr

Jones briefly before heading for home. 'One shot, one goal, that's all it takes sometimes to win a match,' he told them. 'Teams often need a bit of luck in the cup.'

'When's the Final, Mr Jones?' asked Kerry.

'Whoa! Hold your horses,' he chuckled, especially for the benefit of pony-mad Kerry. 'One fence at a time, young lady. We've still got the semi-final to come yet.'

'Yes, I know,' she replied. 'But I'd like to get a medal.'

'Let's hope you will. No reason why not.'

Kerry was about to drop a bombshell on her team's chances of cup glory. 'Well, there is, you see. If the Final's not till after the holidays, it'll be too late,' she explained. 'I'm leaving at Easter!'

2 Out of the Blue

'It's a shame you'll be losing Kerry,' said Grandad on Sunday afternoon.

Chris was gazing through Grandad's kitchen window at the group of lads kicking a ball about on the recreation ground. They were his brother Andrew's mates who had all left primary school the year before.

He nodded in agreement. 'She's the same age as me. We were expecting she'd still be here to play for us next season as well.'

'Didn't anybody know she was leaving?'

'Kerry only found out herself a few days ago. Her parents have just bought a riding school and stables in another county.'

There was a rap on the back door and Andrew burst in – but not as fast as the panting bundle of fur that brushed past his legs.

'Saw Shoot in the garden, so I guessed you'd be here, our kid,' said Andrew as their black and white collie scampered up to Grandad for some fuss. 'Fancy a game of footie with the gang? We need another keeper.'

'Sorry, Mum's sent me out to give him a walk.'

'Who – Grandad or the dog?'

'Cheeky monkey,' Grandad laughed. 'You're right, mind, I could do with a spot of exercise. Go on, off with you both. I'll walk Shoot.'

Grandad followed the brothers out and leant against the garden wall of his cottage to watch them play for a while. Shoot had other ideas. He nosed at his lead that was draped over the wall and looked up, whining.

'OK, OK, I get the message,' chuckled Grandad. 'You win.'

As Grandad set off and threw a stick for the dog to chase, he kept an eye on the footballers. He saw Chris dive low to his left to smother a shot from Tim Lawrence, last year's school team captain.

'Good stop, Chris,' Tim called out. 'I heard about your great display yesterday. Hope you go on to win the cup.'

'Yeah, they might do the double – win the cup and get relegated!' scoffed Andrew. 'League position's a bit dodgy, little brother.'

Chris pulled a face at him. 'We'll stay up, don't worry.'

'Thanks to a girl, maybe,' Andrew chortled. 'You'll have to make sure you play all your games before she goes.'

'We've got Rakesh too – and others. We're not a one-man team.'

'One-girl team you mean!'

Grandad wandered along the bank of the narrow River Dane, amused at Shoot's antics in the water. It wasn't so funny, though, when the dog returned with the stick and shook his fur dry right next to him.

Grandad turned away to protect himself, just in time to see Chris pull off another fine reflex save. 'That's m'boy,' Grandad murmured proudly.

'He's got goalie's blood in his veins, all right. No doubt about that.'

Chris had always wanted to be a goalie. Just like his grandad. Or even perhaps like his dad who used to play in goal for the village team too. Not any more. Tony Weston had left home over three years ago and disappeared abroad. They hadn't seen him since.

Danebridge were back in league action in the first week of March, a home game after school on Wednesday versus local rivals Shenby.

The two schools were always keen to do well against each other, but there was an extra edge to this

match. Shenby were pushing for the league title, while Danebridge were peering anxiously over their shoulders at the relegation zone.

'One thing's for sure,' Mr Jones told the players at their team meeting at morning break. 'If you let Shenby have as many chances as Hanfield, they'll punish you. Don't expect them to be so wasteful.'

'Chris will gobble up anything that gets past us,' Philip grinned, nudging the captain playfully on the arm. 'He's red-hot at the minute.'

'A good job too,' said the headmaster. 'Though I'm sure he'd like to see the other keeper having his hands warmed up as well.'

The match kicked off in blustery conditions, the wind giving Danebridge a first-half advantage as it swept into the faces of the visitors.

Grandad watched from his garden as usual, well muffled in coat, scarf, gloves and cap. Shoot was also there but had no interest in the football. He was eyeing a cat that sat warily on the wall nearby.

Shenby started the stronger, playing neat football into the wind by keeping their passes short and accurate. They seemed much quicker to the ball than Danebridge and Chris was kept busy, grateful to see a snapshot skim wide of the far post.

'C'mon! Get stuck in,' he urged his team. 'They're all over us.'

Philip tried to find Rakesh on the wing with a long, diagonal pass, but not even the swift Rakesh could catch the wind-assisted ball as it ran out of play. The ball was kicked back for a Shenby throw-in by Andrew who had just arrived, still in the

uniform of Selworth Comprehensive.

Shoot began to bark, but it wasn't the usual joyous greeting. It was a warning aimed at the stranger who was with his young master. It alerted Grandad and he held on to the lead more tightly.

If Shoot was alarmed, Grandad was even more so when he looked at the man properly and saw who it was. His son-in-law!

'Hello again, Pop. Long time no see. How are you?'

Tony Weston didn't wait for an answer, nodding towards the Danebridge goalkeeper. 'Nice to see young Chris keeping up the family tradition, eh? Andy tells me Chris is captain too. He must be good.'

'He is,' Grandad stated firmly. 'He'll be better than you or me ever were.'

At that moment, the Shenby number nine was put clean through down the middle with only the goalkeeper to beat.

'Out, Chris, out!' came the loud shout. 'Narrow the angle.'

Chris was distracted by the oddly familiar voice and glanced towards the cottage. He was so shocked, he barely made a move to stop the striker dribbling round him and slotting the ball into the back of the net.

'Why didn't you dive at his feet?' the man yelled as Chris still stared his way. 'You just let him waltz past you.'

Andrew noticed the look of dismay on Grandad's face. 'Er, I think you might have put Chris off a bit there, Dad.'

3 Shoot First...

'What's the matter, Chris?' asked Mr Jones at half-time. 'Are you feeling all right?'

Chris nodded weakly, but his face was as pale as a blank sheet of paper. He kept looking in bewilderment towards the row of cottages and the headmaster followed his gaze, recognizing Mr Weston. 'I didn't know *he* was back on the scene,' he said to himself. 'No wonder the boy's upset.'

Danebridge were now 2-0 down and Chris felt guilty about both goals. The second had trickled between his legs as he took his eye off the ball at the last moment, rattled by another ill-timed bellow from his dad.

As he took up his position in goal for the second half, Dad called to him again. 'C'mon, Chris, wake up! Show them what you're made of.'

'You can't shout out like that at Chris,' Grandad protested to his son-in-law. 'You know he takes things to heart.'

Dad sighed heavily. 'I always did seem to hurt his feelings too easily. Never meant to, I just speak before I think. He'll have to learn that my bark's worse than my bite.'

'Shoot's good at both,' grinned Andrew and then a thought struck him. 'Does Mum know you're here?'

'No, not yet. Might be best for you to tell her first, eh? I don't reckon she'd want me suddenly turning up on the doorstep!'

'You could have warned us all that you were coming,' Grandad remarked. 'How long are you planning on staying?'

'Trying to get rid of me already, are you, Pop?' he grinned, then

answered more seriously. 'Not sure. I need to sort a few things out.'

'Dad picked me up from school in this dead flash car,' Andrew boasted.

'Only hired,' his dad put in. 'But I've got three over in Spain.'

'Three cars! Wow! Are you rich?'

He laughed. 'No, but I'm working on it. Spain's a wonderful country. You'd love it, Andy. Hot sunshine, beaches – great football teams . . .'

'Hold on,' said Grandad. 'Don't go filling his head with all that sort of crazy stuff. He doesn't realize you're joking.'

'No joke, Pop. He's still my son. What's wrong with the idea that he might want to come and live with me instead?'

Shoot picked up the tension between the two men and began to growl again, eyes fixed on the stranger.

'Quiet, Shoot,' ordered Andrew. 'Sorry, Dad. It's just that he doesn't know you yet. Mum bought him for us after you left.'

'She's obviously got him well trained. I don't reckon he likes me.'

'He's got good judgement,' said Grandad stiffly, turning his attention back to the match.

Danebridge were finding it difficult even to get the ball into Shenby's half of the pitch. The combined power of the wind and Shenby's attacks forced them to defend deep, battling away in the hope of keeping the score down. Rakesh and Kerry up front were almost like spectators.

Chris became aware of his dad wandering down the touchline and he tried in vain to keep focused on the game. Dad was soon right behind his goal.

'Hiya, son. How about pulling off a great save for your old dad, eh?'

Chris ignored him, not even turning round.

'C'mon, don't be like that. Haven't seen you for ages.'

'Nearly four years.' Chris was unable to resist pointing that out.

'I send you birthday cards.'

'They're always late. What are you doing back here, anyway?'

'I've come to find out how you're all getting on. Andy was pleased to see me again. And I was hoping you would be too.'

Chris didn't answer. A long, raking pass had split the defence wide open. The ball reached the unmarked left-winger, who had time and space to steady himself and set his sights for a shot at goal.

The ball fizzed to Chris's right, aimed for the gap between him and the post, and he flung himself down low to parry it. The winger was quick to recover and tried to head the rebound over the grounded goalie, but Chris's reactions were just as

sharp. He sprang up and clawed the ball out of the air to turn it aside for a corner. It was a spectacular double save.

'Magic!' Dad praised him. 'I'd have been proud of that in my day.'

Mr Jones held up play. 'I'm sorry, Mr Weston, please don't stand there. Your son needs to have his full concentration on the game.'

'Didn't do too badly just then, did he?' he replied sarcastically.

'Even so,' the headmaster insisted, trying to be polite. 'Please...'

'OK, OK, I'm going. I know when I'm not welcome,' he scowled. 'We'll talk another time, Chris, eh? Get to know each other better.'

He slouched away towards the car park, intending to find a hotel in Selworth. He wasn't expecting an invitation to stay in Grandad's cottage.

Chris felt all churned up inside. Half of him wanted nothing more to do with his dad. The other half wanted to call him back. He caught the headmaster's eye and gave a little helpless shrug.

Mr Jones breathed a sigh and blew his whistle. 'Play on, lads. Play on.'

'How well do you remember Dad?'

Andrew's voice cut through the darkness of the bedroom he shared with his brother. They'd spent all evening discussing their father with Mum, but it hadn't been easy. She still felt bitter about the way that he had deserted them.

'Not as well as you do, it seems,' Chris replied, 'judging by how pally you two were this afternoon, according to Grandad.'

'Well, I'm older than you. You were

only about six when he left, still in the Infants. I was eight. That makes a difference.'

'We're different too. Mum always says I take more after Grandad and that you're more like Dad – but without his good looks!'

Andrew chuckled. 'Can't help it. It's just the way I am, I guess. Shoot first, ask questions later, that's me – even on the soccer pitch!'

'I've noticed. What was Dad like himself in goal, d'you know?'

'Dead loud! He could have shouted for England. You could hear him a mile off yelling things at his team.'

'He hasn't changed much then,' Chris muttered.

'Give him a chance, little brother. He's OK really – just gets a bit carried away at times. We used to have loads of fun together. Remember him playing footie with us in the garden and on the recky?'

'Vaguely. But Dad coming back like this is bound to cause some trouble. He's made me make a mess of things already today.'

'Yeah, what was it in the end, four-nil? You lot were so bad, I reckon you were lucky to get nil! Think you'll avoid getting relegated?'

'Still got three games left. We'll do it,'

Chris said, crossing his fingers under the duvet. 'Kerry's around till Easter.'

Andrew was silent for a minute before he spoke again, somewhat hesitantly. 'Um . . . Kerry might not be the only one on the move. . .'

'How d'you mean?' said Chris, worried about further losses for his team. 'Who else is leaving?'

'Me – maybe.'

'*You!* What are you going on about?'

'Well, I've been thinking about a few things Dad said. Y'know, about Spain. Sounds like a fantastic place to live . . .'

His voice trailed away, testing his brother's reaction. Chris sat bolt upright in bed, trying to make out

Andrew's face to see how serious he was.

'Don't talk stupid. Mum would never let you go off abroad with Dad.'

'How could she stop me?'

Chris was flummoxed for a moment. 'I don't know, but I'm sure she could. There must be some kind of law against it. Like kidnapping.'

'Kidnapping!' Andrew snorted. 'Now who's talking stupid? How can you be kidnapped by your own dad?'

Chris scratched his head. He still thought it wasn't allowed. 'Has Dad actually asked you to go back with him?'

'Not as such,' Andrew admitted.

'No, I bet he doesn't really want to have you cluttering the place up. Besides, you'd miss going on that special coaching course at Easter.'

'Yeah, realized that myself. It

could be my big break, if the coaches there like the look of me.'

'Be an even bigger break here if you did go to Spain,' Chris murmured. 'It'd split the family in two.'

That was the end of their conversation. They didn't even bother to say good night to each other.

4 Family Affairs

The school team squad were back on the recky the following afternoon for their usual Thursday practice session. It was a good chance for them to run the Shenby defeat out of their system.

'Which is more important, d'yer reckon, the league or the cup?' Philip said as he and Chris sat on the grass, tying up their bootlaces before the start. 'I mean, if you had to choose.'

'Both!' answered Chris. 'We still

need a few more league points to be safe, but we also want to win the semi-final next week.'

A football suddenly whistled over their heads and smacked into the wall of the wooden changing hut, making them jump.

'Sorry, guys,' Rakesh laughed. 'I was aiming at you.'

'That's why we're near the bottom of the league,' Philip muttered. 'Our so-called leading scorer can't even hit a couple of sitting ducks!'

After a vigorous warm-up, Mr Jones organized the players into small groups for some much-needed shooting practice. 'You don't have to leave all the scoring up to Rakesh and Kerry, you know,' he told them. 'If you fancy a go at goal, then have a crack. Don't be afraid of missing.'

Chris showed no fear at all when he tried his luck with a few shots as well. He only managed to get one of them on target between the cones.

'Best stick to what you're good at,' grinned Philip.

'Right, I am better at stopping shots,' said Chris. 'Usually.'

'Forget about what happened yesterday. We all have our bad games.'

When Chris returned to goal, he enjoyed his little duel with Rakesh. Out of five efforts, Rakesh only succeeded in beating Chris once. Neither would have admitted it, but they were both counting.

So was Ryan. The youngster was only in Year 4 and he was delighted to put the ball past the captain twice. He'd already scored for the school team as a substitute and the headmaster decided it was about time to name him in the starting line-up.

In the practice match that

followed, Ryan's excellent goal clinched his selection for the semi-final. Kerry was demanding a pass but he had the confidence to go it alone, despite the narrow angle. His shot was as straight as a laser beam, the ball skidding under Chris's dive and scraping the cone on its way in.

'Great strike!' praised Mr Jones before Kerry could moan at Ryan for

not passing. 'If you don't shoot, you don't score – that's what they say in football. And goals are what the game is all about!'

Andrew arrived home later than Chris that evening, enthusing about his own performance in a league match for Selworth's Year 7 side.

'Won six-one!' he bragged to Chris, disturbing his attempts at doing some homework at their bedroom desk. 'Tim got a couple and the poor guy I was marking never had a kick. Apart from a few on his legs, that is!'

'How come they managed to score if you were so brilliant in defence?' muttered Chris as he wrestled with a tricky maths problem.

'Not my fault. Our goalie played a bit like you – useless!'

Chris ignored the taunt, knowing it was just his brother's way of trying to get his attention. Andrew wasn't one to give up easily.

'Dad came to watch me,' he went on. 'Shouted out quite a lot, like he does, but the ref deserved it. Talk about biased. He disallowed about three more of our goals.'

Andrew was becoming frustrated at the lack of response as Mum called them downstairs for tea.

'Don't tell Mum, but I'm full already,' he said, affecting a burp. 'Dad took me and Tim for a Giant Superburger in Selworth.'

'Bribes now, is it?'

'What d'yer mean by that?'

'Nothing,' Chris said innocently. 'Has he bought you a bullfighting outfit as well?'

'Ah, right. I see what you're getting at now,' Andrew sneered. 'No, he hasn't – or a Real Madrid strip either, before you ask.'

Chris stood up from the desk. 'So have you made up your mind about going to sunny Spain?'

His brother gave a shrug. 'Plenty of time. We haven't discussed it yet. Dad's not leaving till he's finished his business here.'

'And what business *is* that exactly?'

Andrew was suddenly serious, dropping his act of bravado. 'It's to do with Mum. She met Dad in town today to talk things over. They've decided to get a divorce.'

'Oh . . .' Chris sat down again with a bump. 'Might have expected it, I suppose. But it still comes as a shock when it actually happens.'

'Come on, boys,' Mum called up once more. 'Your tea's ready. I'm not prepared to wait for ever, you know.'

Danebridge School was gripped by cup fever. They'd been drawn at home in the semi-final against Great Norton.

'If we're on form, we ought to beat them,' said Rakesh as he stuck another poster on the wall outside his classroom. It advertised the big match and appealed for supporters to cheer on the team.

'At least we've avoided Shenby,' Philip piped up, doing the same job further down the corridor. 'They must be the cup favourites.'

Chris admired his pals' artistic efforts. He'd pinned his own on the side of the recky changing hut. 'We'll save Shenby for the Final, with a bit

of luck,' he said. 'We've got a score to settle with them!'

'Yeah, a four-nil one,' Rakesh cackled.

One person who intended to be at the semi-final was Chris's mum.

'The shopping can wait next Saturday,' she told him one teatime. 'If your dad's going to watch the match, like he says, then so shall I.'

'You never went to see me play for Danebridge,' Andrew said sourly.

'I'm not very interested in football, as you well know,' Mum said with a frown. 'You two get all that from Grandad – and your father, of course.'

Chris took Shoot out later for an evening walk around the village to mull things over. He found himself,

almost automatically, at Grandad's cottage. Grandad poured him a cold drink and filled Shoot's bowl with fresh water.

'What's on your mind, m'boy? Problem parents?'

Chris nodded. 'You never know what they'll do next. Both Mum and Dad are going to be at the game. That'll be really weird.'

'Don't worry,' Grandad chuckled. 'I'll be there too, as always. I'll make sure there's no crowd trouble!'

It was said partly in jest, but Grandad knew that football matches tended to bring out the very worst in his impulsive son-in-law. He was expecting fireworks – the kind that suddenly go off bang!

5 Crowd Trouble

'C'mon, ref! That was a corner. Came off a defender.'

The semi-final had only been underway for five minutes when Tony Weston let rip for the first time. He was standing near the halfway line with Andrew, a few metres away from Grandad, Mum and Shoot.

The neutral referee was pointing for a goal-kick to Great Norton and ignored the criticism. Only as he jogged back upfield did he glance warily towards the spectator as the heckling continued.

'Want to borrow some specs, ref?'

There were a few giggles from children nearby, but not many other people in the crowd found the remark very funny. They agreed with the referee that the girl's shot had slithered wide without anyone touching it.

Mr Jones, on the opposite touchline, was far from amused. He knew he might have to take some action soon and put a stop to such nonsense before it affected the players.

Danebridge had made a bright start to the cup-tie. Rakesh had already forced the goalkeeper to make a save and fired another effort just over the crossbar. And now Kerry had gone close too. She was desperate for the team to win today so that she could play in the Final.

'Good try, Kerry!' came Chris's cry of encouragement from the edge of his penalty area. 'We're getting warmer.'

The goal-kick was sliced and Kerry pounced on the loose ball, lofting it back towards goal while the keeper was still out of position. He stumbled and could only watch its flight helplessly, but the ball sailed just a little too high. It thudded against the bar and rebounded down into the boy's arms as he knelt on the ground, as if in prayer.

Gasps of dismay and relief rippled around the touchline from the two sets of supporters before a single voice stood out.

'That's two you've missed inside thirty seconds, girl. You're useless! You shouldn't be on the pitch.'

'You've no right to say something like that,' Mum objected. 'She didn't do it on purpose.'

'Keep your thoughts to yourself, Tony,' Grandad told him sternly. 'That young lass is a fine player.'

He only laughed. 'I don't agree with girls playing football, Pop. Shouldn't be allowed.'

'Shut up, Dad,' Andrew hissed. 'You're not helping. Grandad's right, Kerry's good. She's well worth her place in the team.'

Kerry would have been flabbergasted to hear Andrew sticking up for her. As it was, she glared at the man next to him, wishing that looks could kill. It took all her self control not to shout something rude back.

'Who does that clown in the black jacket think he is?' she stormed at Rakesh. 'Is he one of their lot?'

Rakesh shook his head. 'One of ours, I'm afraid. Hard to believe, but I gather he's Chris's dad.'

'Right!' she answered as realization dawned. 'The guy who went and put Chris off in the league match.'

'That's the one. Nice bloke, eh, by the sound of it!'

It was Danebridge's turn now to do some defending as Great Norton mounted their first raid on Chris's goal. Philip's challenge for the ball was powerful enough to make an attacker lose control before he could shoot – and also lose his balance. The collision of bodies was just outside the penalty area and the referee blew for a direct free-kick.

'That was never a foul!' Dad

screamed. 'The kid fell over his own clumsy feet. You're blind, referee!'

The official shot him a dirty look. 'I'm reffing this game, not you.'

'Yes, and a right mess you're making of it too,' he retorted.

The free-kick was a beauty. The ball was hooked over the defensive wall and slapped into the net well beyond Chris's dive. He had no hope of reaching it in the large recky goals.

His dad was enraged. 'Rubbish, Danebridge! So sloppy. C'mon, Chris, sort your players out. Show 'em who's boss!'

'Don't start on at Chris, Dad,' pleaded Andrew. 'That's not fair.'

Andrew spotted Mr Jones striding round the pitch in their direction. 'Oh, oh!' he muttered under his breath. 'Here comes trouble...'

The headmaster didn't even see Ryan's flying header. Danebridge had almost equalized instantly as Rakesh sped down the wing and curled over a low centre into the goalmouth. It was a wonderful effort from Ryan, the ball flashing only a fraction wide of the far post, but Dad was still cursing another missed chance when he found he had company.

'Please stop shouting things out, Mr Weston,' the headmaster demanded. 'You're embarrassing everybody and making a fool of yourself too.'

'Oh really. It's a free country, isn't it?' he snapped. 'Or at least it was when I left.'

Mum cut in. 'Yes, and I think it's about time you took off again. You're showing us all up.'

His wife's response had the desired effect. It silenced him at last – if only for a while...

Great Norton dominated the rest of the first half, eagerly seeking to increase their 1-0 lead. They were now playing with much more confidence than Danebridge, who seemed to have gone into their shell like a nervous tortoise.

Chris was especially jittery, afraid that any mistake would be picked up by Dad and broadcast to the world. He fumbled a couple of shots he would normally have held comfortably and then dropped a cross at the feet of an attacker. The ball was poked goalwards but Philip scrambled to his captain's rescue by kicking it off the line.

Chris waited for the expected blast and was amazed when it failed to come. He knew Dad was still there. He could see him alongside Mr Jones.

His luck didn't last. Goalkeeping errors are usually costly and so it proved just before the interval. Chris dashed out from his goal to try and catch a corner and mistimed his jump for the ball. It swirled over his

flailing hands and an attacker lurking behind him steered it into the net.

Dad could no longer restrain himself. 'Rubbish, Chris! Get a grip, lad!' he yelled. 'You're letting people down.'

Mr Jones was furious. 'You're the one letting people down, Mr Weston. I must ask you to leave immediately.'

For an awful moment Andrew thought his dad was going to lash out at the headmaster. Dad was clearly having a struggle to control his temper.

'This is a public recreation ground, not your school,' he snarled, refusing to budge. 'I'll stay here as long as I want.'

Shoot sensed the angry mood of the people around him and began barking as Grandad stepped in and put a hand on his son-in-law's arm.

'Time to go,' he said simply, but in a manner that made it plain he meant business. 'Let's have a cup of tea and a chat in my cottage.'

Dad reacted strongly. He snatched his arm away and caught Grandad accidentally across the chest, making him stagger backwards. His cap fell to the ground and only Mum's firm grip on the lead prevented Shoot from launching at her husband.

Andrew did so instead. 'Cool it, Dad!' he cried, yanking him away by his other arm. 'That's enough. You've gone too far.'

His dad suddenly deflated like a burst balloon, shocked that even Andrew had turned against him. He

tried to recover some of his lost dignity, pulling his jacket back into shape and straightening his tie.

'Wasting my time here anyway, watching this shower,' he snorted as a parting shot to Mr Jones. 'They've thrown it away. Danebridge have got no chance now.'

'We might have without you here, Dad,' said Andrew. 'C'mon, let's go.'

6 No Hard Feelings

The half-time whistle blew as Grandad ushered Andrew and his dad into the kitchen. 'Sit down at the table, both of you, while I put the kettle on,' he said. 'We need to have a good talk together.'

So did the Danebridge team. They were losing 2-0, just as against Shenby, and the players rallied round their unhappy captain.

'Nobody's blaming you, Chris,' Philip reassured him. 'You can't help what your dad's like.'

'He's gone now, anyway,' Kerry said. 'Good riddance too!'

'Yeah, just forget about him,' said Rakesh.

Chris wished it was that easy, but at least he tried to shut Dad out of his mind for the moment. 'C'mon, let's put things right where it matters – on the pitch,' he urged his teammates. 'We can still win this game.'

Danebridge staged a spirited comeback at the start of the second half and found the net themselves at last. Kerry set the goal up by dribbling past two defenders and Ryan scored it. As she lost possession of the ball in another challenge, it ran free to Ryan, who squeezed his shot beneath the keeper's dive.

For a while it looked as though an

equalizer was on the cards. Rakesh struck a post and Great Norton were fortunate to withstand several minutes of heavy pressure. Then they caught Danebridge on the break.

The visitors' third goal was almost an exact copy of Danebridge's winner against Hanfield in the previous round. A swift raid up the right wing left Philip having to deal with two pacy opponents at the same time. He couldn't cope and Chris soon had the equally thankless task of picking the ball out of the net.

The semi-final appeared to be all over. And it would have been, too, if Chris hadn't remained alert. Despite the 3-1 scoreline, he felt more relaxed and positive than at any stage in the game, free of further off-field distractions. In a strange sense, Danebridge now had nothing to lose.

'Push forward,' the captain called from the edge of his penalty area. 'All-out attack. We're not gonna be knocked out without a fight.'

The brave tactics nearly backfired immediately. A move broke down after a weak pass and the ball was

punted deep into unguarded Danebridge territory. It even went over the head of Philip, the tallest player on the pitch. As Great Norton's two fastest strikers held a sprint race to see who could reach the ball first, neither of them won. They were beaten to it by Chris, acting as sweeper, who had zoomed out of his area to hack the ball into touch.

'Didn't know you were so quick,' laughed Rakesh.

Chris grinned. 'You'll have to watch out on Sports Day this year!'

The goalkeeper had to repeat his frantic charge out of goal a little later, but this time he miskicked and the winger kept the ball in play. Although Philip delayed the boy's shot long enough for Chris to hare back, the high lob seemed certain to clinch Great Norton's victory.

No-one was quite sure how Chris managed to recover his position in time to fingertip the ball over the bar, but his acrobatics had the crowd gasping. Chris finished up entangled in the netting, too dazed and winded to appreciate the generous applause that rang around the recreation ground.

Danebridge took inspiration from their captain's heroics. They bombarded Great Norton with attack after attack and their opponents eventually cracked in the blitz of raids. Two goals came in three minutes.

Ryan made both of them, slipping accurate passes through the gaps in their defence to allow Rakesh and then Kerry to fire home and bring the scores level at 3-3. The cup-tie had a thrilling climax as Great Norton hung

on for dear life, grateful to survive until the final whistle

'There goes my chance to play in the Final,' sighed Kerry, sitting exhausted on the penalty spot afterwards. 'I bet we won't be able to fit it in now before Easter.'

'We've got to win the replay first,' Rakesh reminded her.

'Oh, we will,' she said confidently. 'I'm sure we'd have won today but for you-know-who. That stupid bloke's gone and cost me my medal!'

Chris was willing to be more forgiving, if only because he realized that Dad's behaviour had helped to bring the best out of his team in the end. Some of the things they'd heard Dad saying had spurred them on even more, determined to prove him wrong.

He collected his clothes from the

hut without bothering to change and followed Mum and Shoot to Grandad's cottage.

'I'm really proud of you,' Mum said. 'It was lovely when everybody was clapping and cheering after that save of yours.'

Chris smiled. 'I'm glad you didn't see us lose, Mum, but it's a shame Dad wasn't there as well. He won't believe how we fought back like that.'

Dad already knew. He'd watched the last part of the game with Andrew and Grandad from a bedroom window and they were all in the kitchen again when Chris opened the door.

'Well played, son,' Dad greeted him. 'Terrific save!'

Andrew laughed at the look of surprise on his brother's face. 'We had a grandstand view from upstairs,' he explained. 'Like being in one of those executive boxes at a soccer stadium.'

'The only problem is, we don't know the final score,' said Grandad. 'You can't have lost, surely, the way people were jumping about.'

Chris shook his head. 'Draw, three each. Replay in a fortnight.'

Dad cleared his throat. 'Er, you'll be pleased to know that I won't be able to spoil things for you then,' he said with a lopsided grin. 'I'm returning to Spain next week.'

'On his own,' Grandad added quickly, as Chris glanced at Andrew.

'I wasn't really planning on going, anyway,' he said, trying to sound casual. 'I'd miss everybody here too

much – even you, our kid!'

Shoot wandered over to sit at Dad's side, yawned and waited to be stroked. 'Typical!' grunted Dad, tickling the dog's ears. 'Shoot's decided we can be friends now that I'm leaving.'

'Perhaps he doesn't see you as a threat any more,' said Mum. 'It'd be nice if we could all try and be friends again.'

'Even join you in Spain for a holiday?' suggested Andrew hopefully.

'You'd be very welcome to,' Dad said. 'No hard feelings, eh, Chris? Sorry about my big mouth.'

'No hard feelings, Dad,' Chris replied, smiling. 'At least my team know it's big enough for them to make you eat all your words!'

Dad laughed loudly. 'And I know that Danebridge have got a top class keeper. Their future's in safe hands – so long as I'm not around!'

Shoot slumped down at their feet, curled up and dozed off. Some things in life, seemed to be his message, were far more important than what happened on a football field – even during a cup semi-final!

THE END